Betty Ford
WOMEN'S RIGHTS AND HEALTH ADVOCATE

BY ALYSSA KREKELBERG

Published by The Child's World®
1980 Lookout Drive • Mankato, MN 56003-1705
800-599-READ • www.childsworld.com

Photographs ©: AP Images, cover, 1, 16; Library of Congress, 5; Everett Collection/
Newscom, 6, 11; Courtesy Gerald R. Ford Library, 8, 12; MSG/AP Images, 14; Dave
Buresh/Denver Post/Getty Images, 19; Everett Collection Historical/Alamy, 20

Copyright © 2018 by The Child's World®
All rights reserved. No part of this book may be reproduced or utilized in any form or
by any means without written permission from the publisher.

ISBN 9781503823945
LCCN 2017944732

Printed in the United States of America
PA02362

ABOUT THE AUTHOR

Alyssa Krekelberg is a children's book editor and author. She lives
in Minnesota.

TABLE OF CONTENTS

Fast Facts 4

Chapter 1
Surviving Cancer 7

Chapter 2
Fighting for Women's Rights 13

Chapter 3
Lasting Legacy 17

Think About It 21
Glossary 22
Source Notes 23
To Learn More 24
Index 24

FAST FACTS

Full Name
- Elizabeth "Betty" Anne Bloomer Ford

Birthdate
- April 8, 1918, in Chicago, Illinois

Husband
- President Gerald R. Ford Jr.

Children
- Michael, John, Steven, and Susan

Years in the White House
- 1974–1977

Accomplishments
- Spoke publicly about her breast cancer **treatment** when diagnosed in 1974.
- Helped to raise awareness for women's health across the country.

- Worked hard for women's rights, including supporting the Equal Rights **Amendment**.
- Helped create the Betty Ford Center in 1982, which has helped more than 90,000 people fight their **addiction** to drugs.

Chapter 1

SURVIVING CANCER

Betty Ford stepped carefully from the helicopter. She took a deep breath and let the autumn air fill her lungs. It was a welcome change from the stale hospital smell that had surrounded her for the past two weeks. Her husband, Gerald, stood beside her. He offered his arm as they made their way toward the White House.

Betty was tired from her recent surgery. But she was grateful the doctors had caught her breast cancer and saved her life. Although she had been the First Lady for only two months, the country had supported her. Betty received more than 50,000 pieces of mail from well-wishers.

◀ Betty Ford was all smiles when she left the hospital after her cancer treatment in 1974.

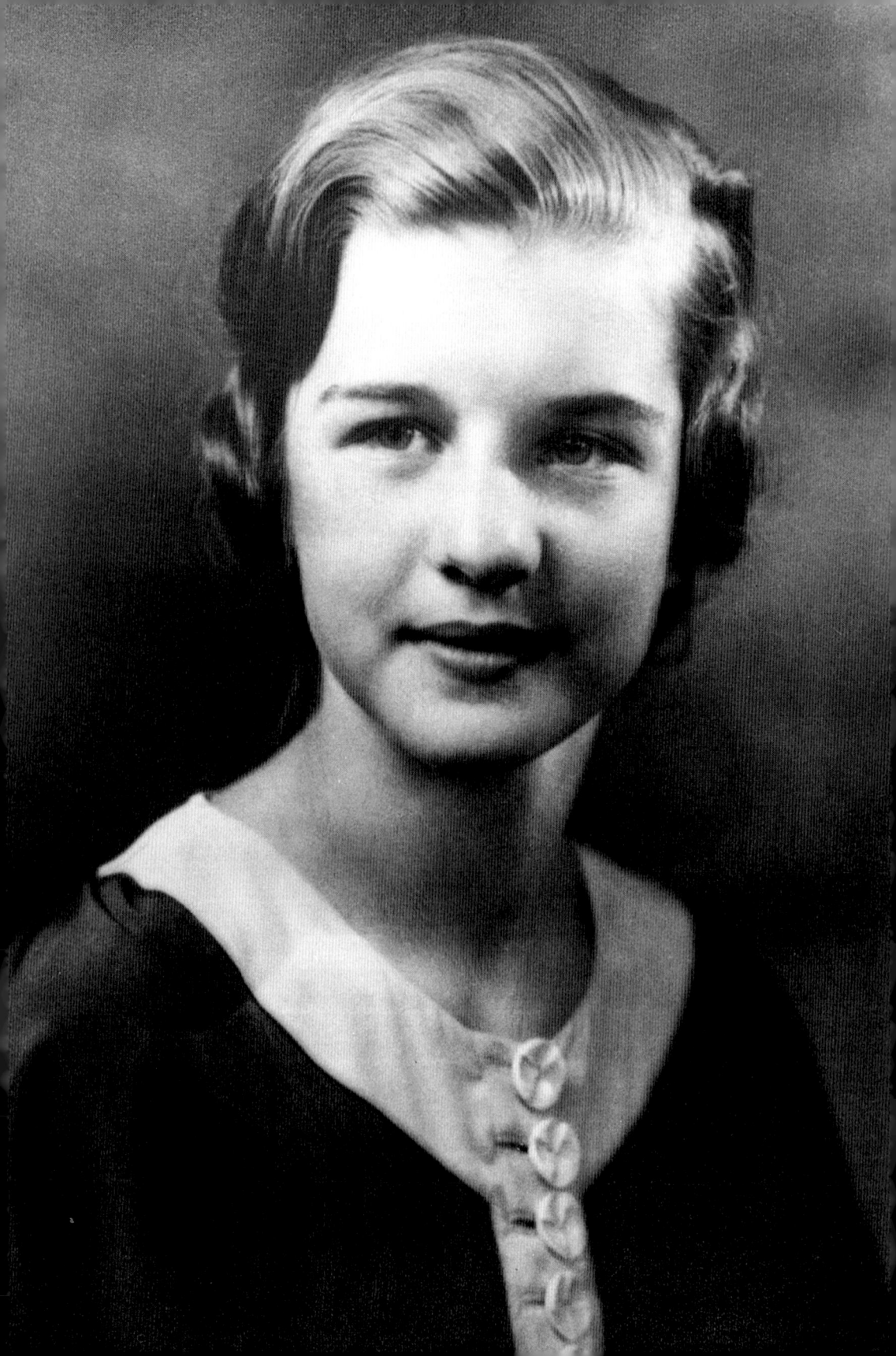

As Betty and Gerald approached the White House that autumn day in 1974, she was showered with more support. The entire White House staff was lined up by the entrance. Some held signs saying, "We Love You, Betty."

Throughout her recovery, Betty spoke publicly about her cancer. At this time, cancer was a topic most people avoided. But her willingness to talk about it caused thousands of women to visit their doctors to get **screened** for the disease. Betty realized she could help women across the country. "Thinking of all those women going for cancer checkups because of me, I'd come to recognize more clearly the power of the woman in the White House. Not *my* power, but the power of the position, a power which could be used to help."[1]

Betty never imagined she would someday become the First Lady. When she was young, she dreamed of becoming a dancer.

◀ **Betty at the age of 14**

Betty was born in 1918 and raised in Grand Rapids, Michigan. When she was 29 years old, Betty met Gerald through a friend. They fell in love and married in 1948. Then, Gerald was elected to Congress for the first time.

Betty and Gerald packed up their belongings and moved to Washington, DC, where Gerald served in Congress for the next 25 years.

Everything changed when President Richard Nixon **appointed** Gerald as his vice president in 1973. When Nixon was caught in a public scandal eight months later, he **resigned** as president. The Ford family suddenly found themselves in a position they had never expected. On August 9, 1974, Gerald was sworn in as the 38th president of the United States. As he took the oath of office, Betty stood smiling by his side. She was shocked that her life had taken this unexpected turn. But she was ready to begin her role as the First Lady.

Gerald was the first vice president to take office because the president had resigned. ▶

Chapter 2

FIGHTING FOR WOMEN'S RIGHTS

Betty looked at the long list lying before her. The names and phone numbers of legislators were printed in dark ink. She picked up the phone and began dialing. As the phone rang, she stared out the window over the White House lawn. She twirled the spiral phone cord between her fingers. Betty knew what she had to say to the politicians on the other end of the line. She was ready to fight for a cause she believed in wholeheartedly.

In the 1970s, women's rights groups wanted politicians to support the Equal Rights Amendment. This amendment to the Constitution would make men and women equal under the law.

◀ Betty was thrilled when Gerald created a national commission to recognize the International Women's Year in 1975.

▲ In June 1976, a child wrote a letter to Gerald asking why women can't be equal. Betty held up the letter at a women's event.

Betty was a strong **advocate** for the Equal Rights Amendment. She spent many long hours at her desk. Betty wrote numerous letters to legislators about why they should show their support for the amendment. She traveled to different states and gave speeches on the importance of equality between men and women.

"Many barriers continue to block the paths of most women, even on the most basic issue of equal pay for equal work," Betty said to a crowd in Cleveland, Ohio, in 1975.[2] They cheered at her words. Because of her work, Betty was named one of *Time* magazine's Women of the Year in 1975.

Betty was not afraid to speak up for what she believed in. She often spoke to the media about topics that were not discussed publicly, such as her support for the Supreme Court's decision to give women access to certain types of health care services. Betty knew some people disapproved of her opinions. But she refused to change how she acted.

"I tried to be honest; I tried not to dodge subjects. I felt the public had a right to know where I stood. Nobody had to feel the way I felt, I wasn't forcing my opinions on anybody, but if someone asked me a question, I gave that person a straight answer."[3]

—Betty Ford

Chapter 3

LASTING LEGACY

Betty sat on the couch in her home in Palm Springs, California, in 1978. She looked at the concerned faces of her children and husband sitting around her. They told her they were worried about her. She had developed an addiction to alcohol and prescription pills. Her family wanted her to get help.

Betty knew they were right. She wanted to stop using drugs, but her body was dependent on them. So she packed some clothes and checked into a treatment center. There, she received counseling to help overcome her addiction.

Betty was no longer the First Lady. Gerald had lost the presidential election to Jimmy Carter in 1976.

◂ Gerald and their four children supported Betty through her struggles with addiction.

Betty used her position as former First Lady to help educate the country on addiction. Betty helped reduce the shame people had about their addictions. And she got the country talking about the subject. Betty worked hard to show people that recovery from this disease was possible.

> "I . . . had breast cancer and I had survived that. And now I was confronted with addiction. And . . . I made up my mind I was going to survive that, too."[5]
>
> —Betty Ford

She also wanted to directly help the millions of people in the country who were suffering from drug dependency. So, in 1982, Betty **cofounded** a **nonprofit** treatment center called the Betty Ford Center. She ran the facility and spoke with people who came there. She was not ashamed to say, "Hi, my name is Betty, and I'm an alcoholic."[4] She was proud of the work her center did every day.

After her time in treatment, Betty encouraged women to get the same help she did. ▶

18

Tens of thousands of people have received help at the Betty Ford Center to overcome their dependency on drugs. In 2014, the Betty Ford Center merged with another treatment center, Hazelden. Today, it is known as the Hazelden Betty Ford Foundation. It is known as one of the best treatment centers in the world. It is Betty's lasting legacy to the country.

THINK ABOUT IT

- Betty was not afraid to talk about subjects that made people uncomfortable. How did her openness help create change?
- Betty is known as an outspoken and honest First Lady. Do you believe the president's spouse should use his or her position to promote causes he or she believes in?
- During her lifetime, Betty did many things to help people. What do you think people should remember most about her?

◂ Betty Ford died on July 8, 2011. The Betty Ford Center is still a well-known treatment center today.

GLOSSARY

addiction (uh-DIK-shun): An addiction is a dependency on a drug. Betty had an addiction to alcohol and prescription pills.

advocate (AD-vuh-kit): An advocate is someone who publicly supports a cause. Betty was an advocate for women's rights.

amendment (uh-MEND-muhnt): An amendment is a change that is made to a law or document. Betty supported the Equal Rights Amendment, which would help women gain more rights.

appointed (uh-POINT-ed): To be appointed is to be assigned a job. Gerald was appointed vice president.

cofounded (co-FOUND-ed): To have cofounded something is to be one of the founders of an organization. Betty cofounded the Betty Ford Center.

nonprofit (non-PROF-it): A nonprofit is an organization that does not make money from its services. The Betty Ford Center is a nonprofit.

resigned (ri-ZINED): Someone who resigned has given up a job or position. After Nixon resigned, Gerald became the president.

screened (SKREEND): To be screened is to be tested for a disease. Betty encouraged women to get screened for cancer.

treatment (TREET-munt): Treatment is the medical care a patient receives for an illness. Betty created a treatment center for people with a dependency on drugs.

SOURCE NOTES

1. Betty Ford. *The Times of My Life.* New York, NY: Harper & Row: 1978. Print. 212.

2. "First Lady Betty Ford's Remarks to the International Women's Year Conference." *Ford Library Museum.* Gerald R. Ford Presidential Library and Museum, n.d. Web. 24 July 2017.

3. Betty Ford. *The Times of My Life.* New York, NY: Harper & Row: 1978. Print. 223.

4. Nancy Gibbs. "Betty Ford, 1918–2011." *Time.* Time, 8 July 2011. Web. 24 July 2017.

5. "Betty Ford, First Lady of Recovery Advocacy." HazeldenBettyFord.org. *Hazelden Betty Ford Foundation*, n.d. Web. 24 July 2017.

TO LEARN MORE

Books
House, Katherine L. *The White House for Kids.* Chicago, IL: Chicago Review Press, 2014.

Krull, Kathleen. *A Kids' Guide to America's First Ladies.* New York, NY: HarperCollins, 2017.

Pastan, Amy. *First Ladies.* New York, NY: DK Publishing, 2017.

Web Sites
Visit our Web site for links about Betty Ford:
childsworld.com/links

Note to Parents, Teachers, and Librarians: We routinely verify our Web links to make sure they are safe and active sites. So encourage your readers to check them out!

INDEX

addiction, 17–18
alcoholic, 18
Betty Ford Center, 18, 21
breast cancer, 7
Carter, Jimmy, 17
drugs, 17, 21

Equal Rights Amendment, 13, 14
Ford, Gerald, 7, 9–10, 17
Grand Rapids, Michigan, 10
Nixon, Richard, 10

Palm Springs, California, 17
Supreme Court, 15
Time magazine, 15
treatment center, 17–18, 21
White House, 7, 9, 13